The
WITCHES
of
BENEVENTO

The WITCHES of BENEVENTO

JOHN BEMELMANS MARCIANO
and SOPHIE BLACKALL

RESPECT YOUR GHOSTS

A Sergio Story

VIKING

VIKING

An imprint of Penguin Random House LLC

375 Hudson Street

New York, New York 10014

First published in the United States of America by Viking,
an imprint of Penguin Random House LLC, 2017

LIBRARY OF CONGRESS CATALOGING-IN-PUBLICATION DATA IS AVAILABLE.

ISBN 9780451471833

1   3   5   7   9   10   8   6   4   2

Manufactured in China   Set in IM FELL French Canon
Book design by Nancy Brennan

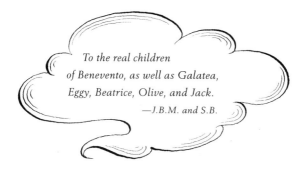

*To the real children
of Benevento, as well as Galatea,
Eggy, Beatrice, Olive, and Jack.*

—J.B.M. and S.B.

CONTENTS

OPENING NOTE 1

MAP OF BENEVENTO 4

1   *Shopping* 11

2   *Home* 19

3   *Promise Not to Tell, Part I* 27

4   *Promise Not to Tell, Part II* 41

5   *Catch a Janara by the Hair* 59

6   *Vendetta* 71

7   *The Boat* 81

8   *The House of Carrozzo* 95

9   *Beloved Ancestors* 105

10 *Home Sweet Home* 115

CLOSING NOTE 128

SPEAKING WITH HANDS 130

HOW THEY LIVED 132

HISTORICAL NOTE 134

Dear, dear Reader,

Once there was a man who left Benevento to go to America. He loved the New World, but there was ONE thing he never could get used to: the lack of spirits.

He expected America to have no Janara or Manalonga or Cloppers—maybe even no demons (perish the thought!)—but no SPIRITS? That was like having a night sky with no stars!

This man (a soldier—you may know him) missed the fairies and sprites who dwell in woods and

Rivers, but most of all He missed the spirits that live in Houses.

A House spirit can be a sprite who lives in the Rafters or the ghost of an ancestor. Such spirits are considered marks of good fortune, and not _ever_ to be taken for granted. Benevento is littered with abandoned Homes whose occupants didn't take proper care of their spirits.

So please, no matter How unpleasant their Requests may be, always, ALWAYS Heed your spirits and give them their daily offerings. Otherwise, you may find yourself looking for somewhere else to live, like the poor, confused lad whose tale now begins.

YOUR DEAR FRIEND,
SIGISMONDO
(WITH BRUNO AND RAFAELLA)

THE WITCHES
of
BENEVENTO

*When you hear the Clopper's **clop clop clop**,*

Run through the Theater and never stop.

Keep far from Bridges and from Wells,

Where Manalonga love to dwell.

If you are good and do your chores,

The Janara won't get you while you snore.

Respect your Ghosts and love your Sprites,

Kiss your Mom and say Good Night.

RESPECT YOUR GHOSTS

A Sergio Story

1.

SHOPPING

RIGHT now, Sergio has a problem.

He needs eggs. Not for himself, not for his mom, but for his household spirit.

Lots of people in Benevento have such spirits, like the girl down the street who has a fairy living under the bed. Sergio's spirit, however, is not a sprite or fairy but a ghost. People become ghosts when they die before they should. But that's a whole *other* story.

Sergio's problem is that, with all the Janara mischiefs, there have been no eggs, and this makes his ghost mad. Bis-Bis *loves* eggs.

Up, up, up the hill Sergio trudges, past the baker's, past the Carrozzos', under the arch, until he gets to Primo's grocery stand.

"Sorry, no eggs," Primo says.

"But I thought the Twins had gotten rid of their mischiefs!" Sergio says.

"They did," Primo says, shrugging. "But they haven't come yet today."

Dang. Now Sergio has to go all the way to the Twins' farm!

Down, down, down the hill Sergio walks, and breaks into a run when he gets to the Theater. (*He* isn't going to get caught by the Clopper like Maria Beppina!) Through the city gate, he slows down to give the horns and spit, to ward off

Malefix, the nasty spirit who lives there.

At the bridge he's off running again, singing **LA-la-la-la-LA!** at the top of his lungs, so as not to hear the Manalonga.

By the time he gets to the Twins', he's all sweaty. When did it get so warm, anyway?

"Do you have any eggs?" Sergio asks.

"We have *so* many eggs!" Rosa says proudly. "We are up to our EARS in eggs! That's why we're late making deliveries—we have too *much* stuff to load up! Just look at this friarielli!"

"Nice," Sergio says, taking a big bunch of leafy greens from her.

"And we're the *only* ones," Rosa says. "Everybody else is still getting mischiefed except us, because **I** stopped the Janara."

"Do you *still* think your doggie doodles had anything to do with ending the mischiefs?" Emilio says to his sister as he places another crate of eggs in the ox cart.

"Doggie doo–doo?" Sergio says.

"*Doodles,* he said!" Rosa says. "And they weren't doodles, they were *drawings.* Darn good ones, too!"

"For a four-year old, maybe," Emilio says.

"Well it sure wasn't the oregano your *mystery* person told you to rub everywhere that chased them away!" Rosa says, hands on hips.

Rosa is furious at her brother for not telling

her who his "mystery person" is, but right now Sergio doesn't care. He takes the eggs and friarielli and leaves the Twins arguing.

Back home, Sergio prepares the morning offering for his ghost. But, dang! He forgot to get candles. Bis-Bis is going to be furious.

"Sergio!" his mom yells from the other room. "I need you to go get bread!"

"But *Mom*, I have to finish—"

"Now!"

Back up, up, up the hill Sergio goes to the baker's. Inside, he orders two loaves, one for his mom and one for Bis-Bis.

"How *is* your ghost?" the baker's daughter asks, getting him the bread.

Sergio complains about all the offerings he has to make.

"You have to do all *that*?" she says. "Why, our little oven sprite barely wants anything! We just sprinkle a little flour in each corner of the room and Cicilia is *so* happy. And helpful! Our bread tastes better every day."

"Is this kid whining about his ghost again?"

Into the shop walks Mozzo, Sergio's least favorite person in the world. But then, he's a Carrozzo, and everyone hates the Carrozzos. Well, everyone except Sergio's mom. But that's *another* other story.

The Carrozzos are the wealthiest family in the Triggio, and all because—some say—of the ghost who lives with them. (Sergio wishes *his* ghost would make him rich!)

"I don't know what he's always complaining for," Mozzo says. "We're happy to take care of *our* ghost, and he's happy to take care of us!"

As the two of them go on about how great their spirits are, Sergio grabs the loaves and leaves. He'd rather be anywhere but here. Even home.

2
HOME

"WHERE have you **been**!?"

Bis-Bis is roaring with hunger and fury the moment Sergio opens the door.

"Do you have **no** idea what time it is? Were you going to make me wait **all day** to eat? Do you not even **care** about your ancestors?"

Bis-Bis is Sergio's great-great-great-great-great-grampa, who died in the earthquake of 1688, but not quite enough. He's what you call an ancestor spirit, and Sergio has to look after his needs because Sergio is Bis-Bis's last remaining descendent living in the house.

This *should* be a good thing. Ghosts—and house spirits generally—are supposed to be helpful, like Mozzo's is. *Those* ghosts let their relatives in on the secrets of the Underworld and stuff, which is what leads to them being so filthy rich. Bis-Bis, on the other hand, just tells boring stories about when he was alive.

"Look!" Sergio says. "Eggs! I had to go all the way to the Twins'. And I made them just how you like."

"**Bah!**" Bis-Bis says, making a sour face as he bites into one egg. "These are **too** hard-boiled." This doesn't stop him from finishing it though. Or eating two more.

"This salt is too **clumpy**! This bread is too **soft**! Where's the **pepper**?"

Even as he complains, Bis-Bis is gobbling it all up. "And you call **this** friarielli?"

"You're lucky I was able to get you anything at all!" Sergio says. "The Twins are the only ones with friarielli *or* eggs because of how bad the mischiefs are this year."

"**Mischiefs!** You complain about **mischiefs**!" Bis-Bis says, his mouth full. "Back in my day, the Janara were **really** bad. But did **we** complain about them? No we did **not**!"

Does Mozzo have to put up with any of this? Sergio wonders.

"And what's that **noise** going on outside?" Bis-Bis says. "I can hardly enjoy my **offering**!"

Sergio opens the shutter to look. Primo and his family are

moving all their furniture into the street.

"Hey, what's going on?" he hollers down.

"It's a party!" Primo yells up.

"What did he say?" the ghost asks.

"Oh, nothing," Sergio says, locking the shutter. Bis-Bis *hates* parties.

After licking his plate clean, the ghost burps, farts, and burps again. Sergio has to breathe through his mouth to keep out the stink. *Skeevo!*

Taking advantage of his ghost's food-induced stupor, Sergio excuses himself—"I must be going now"—and escapes out the door.

As he closes it, Bis-Bis roars, "Hey, where are my **candles**?" but Sergio pretends not to hear.

Down the outside stairs, Sergio arrives at his own door to the sound of crying babies.

Bad sign.

"Hey, Sergio, come on over!" Primo yells from across the street. "The band just started playing! They're amazing!"

"*Sergio!* Is that you?" his mother yells from inside. "Why are you waiting at the door like an idiot? Come inside right now!"

Sergio's mother is *always* complaining about him. About his being lazy, about his being stupid, and about the way he is always fussing over his ghost when it is really his poor mother (herself) and three baby brothers he should be worried about.

"Hey, Mom," Sergio says, walking in. "Can I go over to Primo's? They're having a party."

His mother looks at him like he's lost his mind.

"You are not going ANYwhere until you clean up this place! Do you not see that bowl on the ground? Pick it up!" she says. "And that spoon! Don't leave it lying there!"

As she orders Sergio to clean the house item by item, his stepfather arrives home for supper, dressed in his town crier outfit. He places his trumpet on the ground, perches his hat atop it, and pours himself a glass of wine.

He doesn't say a word, but Sergio's step-dad never says a word, except when he is yelling the news all over town. He does, however, give Sergio a look of bedraggled solidarity that says: *I know. Believe me, I know. . . .*

3
PROMISE NOT TO TELL,
PART I

THE next morning starts badly, with Sergio rolling over on the table where he sleeps and getting poked in the ribs with a knife someone left there at dinner. It gets worse, with Bis-Bis complaining about the party keeping him up all night, and worser still when Sergio finds his mom filling a sack with stinky diapers. Then—

"OW!" Sergio says as Sessimo bites him on the leg. "Why, you little—!"

"Sergio! Be nice to your little brother!" his mother says. "He's just a baby!"

Settimo, lying in the basket he sleeps in, takes his big toe out of his mouth to gurgle-giggle at Sergio's pain. Which he does again when Quinto kicks him in the shin.

This is what Sergio has to put up with every day from his three little half-brothers. Sergio has three older brothers, too—full brothers—but they left home as soon as they were old enough to become shepherds, like their father was. Sergio can't wait for the day *he* is old enough to go away, too.

"Make sure you do both sacks of laundry *and* the basket," Momma says.

Sergio manages to hold one sack in front of him and sling the other across his back while balancing the basket on his head.

With his bad eyesight, Sergio can't see more than a few steps ahead of himself usually, and with the bag in front of him it's even less. He tries to steer clear of everyone crissing and crossing the Theater, but he can't, and he bumps into someone. Both bags and the basket spill to the ground.

"Watch where you're going, kid!" the man he walked into says angrily. He gives Sergio the mundza, a gesture that isn't very nice. (At least it wasn't a *two*-handed mundza.)

Now Sergio has to pick the caca diapers up off the muddy and manurey street, with people passing him holding their noses.

"Ha-ha! Look at the **loser**!"

Sergio lifts his head to see Mozzo Carrozzo pointing and laughing as he drives by in a mule cart. The spinning wheel tosses up a wet sheet of manure-mud into Sergio's face.

Boy, does he hate those Carrozzos!

Down at the river, everyone is already doing their laundry: the Twins with their little brother, Dino; Primo with his big sister, Isidora; and—thank Plutone!—Maria Beppina. She usually helps Sergio with the laundry. (In fact, she usually kinda does it for him.)

They are all talking about how much fun they had at the party last night. Not Sergio. When he finally *did* get there, he spent most of the time hiding so he wouldn't have to dance.

"I had a little *too* much fun," Maria Beppina says, yawning. "I have to go home and take a nap."

"You aren't going to help me?" Sergio says as sweetly as he can.

Maria Beppina smiles. And leaves.

Dang! Now he has to do all these diapers *by himself.*

After lackadaisically rinsing a couple of them, however, Sergio gets bored and starts looking for river treasures.

Hidden under the rabbit hutch in his back garden, Sergio keeps a box of things he has found in the river.

BOTTLE DOLPHIN BONE ARROW PUPPET HEAD BROKEN BIT OF A DISH

"You're wasting your time," Primo says in a brag. "You'll never find *anything* as good as the ring!"

Last week, Primo discovered a gold ring inside of a fish. It is without a doubt the greatest thing anyone has ever found in the river—puppet heads included. Sergio *wishes* he could have it for his box. What makes it even *more* amazing is that the ring is magic.

"Hey, isn't it *my* turn to wear the ring?" Rosa says loudly. "After all, **I** am the one who caught the fish you found it in."

"No way!" Primo says. "It was my idea to look inside the fish and and so it's *my* ring. You'd just lose it, anyway. Or sell it."

"Would not!"

"Would too!"

"Does anyone want to come mushroom picking with me?" Emilio asks, interrupting Primo and Rosa's bickering. "Zia Giltruta is paying two quattrini per orange monkey button, and *five* for any spotted toadstools."

"Ugh," Rosa says. "Mushroom hunting is the dorkiest, lamest thing ever! I'm not missing lunch to pick fungus!"

"Me neither," Dino says, copying Rosa.

"Well, count *me* in!" Primo says.

"No, count *you* out," Isidora says. "Poppa wants us to go collect firewood today, remember?"

"Ahhh ..." Primo says, giving a silly googly-eyed look and falling backward into the water. Dino laughs. Of course, Dino laughs at everything Primo does.

Isidora shakes her head in disgust.

"Well, I'll do it!" Sergio says. He could use some money.

"Let's go," Emilio says, tossing a sack of clean laundry onto his back to take home.

Sergio will deal with the diapers later.

"There's a good one!" Emilio says, heading deeper into the woods. He walks about a hundred feet, squats down, and snatches a mushroom. "Yep, that's worth two quattrini right there!"

How can Emilio *see* that far? Sergio has to squint just to see his toenails.

While Emilio drops it in his almost-full bucket, Sergio looks down into his shirt,

which he is holding up like a pouch. He's got three mushrooms.

"Are you *sure* you know where we are?" he says. They've been climbing in the woods for hours, and Sergio couldn't find his way home if his life depended on it.

"Sure I'm sure," Emilio says.

Sergio's heart skips a beat as he sees a little glimpse of orange on the side of a log. "A monkey button!" he says. "I found one!"

Emilio comes over to inspect. "Nope," he says, shaking his head. "That one's poisonous! It's got to have orange on the under part of the mushroom, not the top."

Who ever knew picking mushrooms would be this hard? And boring. Rosa was right.

They come to a stream where Emilio cups his hands to get a drink of water. Mischief Season really must finally be over, because there's mint growing on the bank. Sergio pinches a leaf and sniffs it.

"Why do Janara like the smell of oregano?" Sergio asks. "Mint smells so much better!"

"They like what they like," Emilio says, shrugging.

"But how do you *know* that that's what they like?"

"Because someone told me," Emilio says, getting annoyed, or agitated, or something.

"The 'mystery person,' right?" Sergio says. "But how do *they* know? And how do you *know* they know?"

"Because he's a Janara!" Emilio blurts out.

"He's a *Janara*!" Sergio says. "For *real*?"

Emilio smacks himself on the forehead. "I *shouldn't* have told you that!"

HE'S A JANARA!

I SHOULDN'T HAVE TOLD YOU THAT!

"Who is it?" Sergio says. "Come on, you've **got** to tell me!"

"There's no *way* I can tell you who it is! I'd get into big trouble. *He'd* get into big trouble! But . . ." Emilio says, stopping himself. "He did tell me something *else*. A secret. A BIG secret."

"A secret? What is it?" Sergio says. "Come on, you can't just tell me you have a secret and then not tell me what it is!"

"If I tell you, do you **promise** not to tell anyone else?"

"I **promise!**"

"Okay," Emilio says, looking around to see if anyone's here. But who could be here? Sergio has no idea where here even *is*.

"Someone we know is a Janara," Emilio whispers. "Because one of us is *living* with a Janara!"

"What?" Sergio says. "Are you *sure*?"

"That's what this person told me," Emilio says. "And he was right about the oregano."

Sergio can't **believe** it! One of them, *living* with a Janara—could it really be true?

"Who do you think it is?" he says.

"I don't know. It could be anybody!" Emilio says. "Well, anybody except Dino, I guess. And your little brothers."

That was for sure. Demons, maybe, but not Janara.

Sergio gets a shiver. He looks up and sees a cloud passing over the sun.

"Do you think Janara are doing *that*?" Sergio says, pointing up at the roaming cloud. Some people say Janara don't like being talked about and will turn the weather bad if you do.

Emilio looks up. "Nah, it's just the wind," he says. "How many mushrooms have you got?"

Sergio looks in his shirt. "Three."

"Two," Emilio says, plucking one of them out.

Sergio squints, trying to see what's wrong with it.

"Don't worry, we're in it together, even-steven," Emilio says. "I'll get the money from Zia Giltruta and stop by in the morning with your half."

Heading home, Sergio can't stop thinking about the money. And the secret! One of them *lives* with a Janara! This is big news—the BIG-GEST. He has to go tell Primo! Oh, *wait*. Dang! He can't! It's a secret. He keeps forgetting. Which reminds him—the candles! Bis-Bis will be *furious* if he forgets the candles again!

But Sergio is forgetting something else, too.

4

PROMISE NOT TO TELL,
PART II

". . . AND there were *twenty* soldiers guarding
the mule train. It was carrying the month's pay
for the entire army, with one chest of silver
coins and another of gold. *Then*, right as they
rounded the mountain into the Forks, ***BAM!*** Il
Diavolino and his men ambushed them!"

Sergio gulps. Witches are one thing, but
bandits are *really* scary.

"*If anyone makes a move, I'll cut his head
off!*" Zì Filippo says in a throaty voice, snip-
ping a wick and letting two candles drop into a
bag. "That's what Il Diavolino told them. Then
he took everything. The silver, the gold, the
mules—even their clothes—and left the whole

regiment standing naked on the highway. Then his whole band disappeared—*POOF!*—back into the mountains."

As he hands Sergio the bag, the candle-maker says in a whisper, "They say Il Diavolino has a vendetta against the army paymaster and *that's* why he attacked them!"

A *vendetta* is an argument that never ends. It can be over something important—like a murder—or over the littlest insult, like not doffing your cap. Bandits always have vendettas, but so do lots of people in Benevento.

Imagining he's a bandit making his get-away with a sack of silver and gold, Sergio heads home with the bag of candles under his arm. When he gets there, he opens the door as quietly as he can, to avoid his mother hearing him and giving him something *else* to do.

Creeping, he sees Primo holding Settimo and singing him a nursery rhyme.

That's strange, Sergio thinks, and makes a loud noise to alert Primo he's there.

RESPECT YOUR GHOSTS
AND LOVE YOUR SPRITES
KISS YOUR MOM...

Primo fast puts
down the naked baby,
who crawls away.

"Isidora is so *weird*!"
Primo says. "The
whole time we were
collecting wood
she wouldn't even
speak. She's the
total opposite of fun."

While Primo goes on
and on—he always com-
plains about his sister—
all Sergio can think
about is how much he
wants to tell him The
Secret. Since he can't,

Sergio tries his best *not* to think about it. But how can you not think about something you are trying so hard not to think about? It's like trying not to picture a bear wearing a hat. See? You just did!

"Anyway, forget my dumb sister," Primo says. "How was mushroom hunting with Emilio?"

"I didn't go mushroom hunting with Emilio," Sergio says, not wanting to give anything away.

"What are you talking about?" Primo says. "I *saw* you go off with Emilio."

"Oh, yeah, I *did*," Sergio says, trying to think quick. "But there weren't any mushrooms, so I left right away."

Primo gives him a look of disbelief. "I *just* ran into Emilio, and he was holding a huge basket of mushrooms. He said you guys were out picking for *three* hours!"

"Uh . . ." Sergio says.

Primo squints at Sergio. "Are you hiding something from me? A secret?'

"No, I'm not hiding a secret," Sergio says nervously, and scratches the back of his neck.

"**A-ha!**" Primo says. "You *always* scratch the back of your neck when you're lying! What's the secret? Come on, give it up!"

"No, I can't!" *Whoops*, Sergio thinks. "I mean, there *is* no secret!"

"Let's see . . ." Primo says, tapping his chin. "It's got to be something that happened while you were with Emilio. Or something Emilio *told* you. Is it about the oregano?"

The way Primo looks at Sergio, it's like he's seeing right *inside* of him.

"He told you who told him, didn't he?" Primo says. "So who is it? Who's the mystery man?"

"I don't know, I swear!" Sergio says. "Emilio

wouldn't tell me who told him about the oregano or anything."

"*What* 'or anything'?" Primo says. "Come on, spill it!"

The thing is, Sergio really *wants* to tell Primo, even though he knows he'll get into trouble for it at some point.

"Do you promise not to tell *anyone* else?" Sergio says. "Especially not Rosa?"

"I promise!"

"Okay," Sergio says. "The person who told Emilio about the oregano is a *real* live Janara." Sergio stops, looks around, and covers his mouth. "And the crazy thing is," he whispers, "he said that one of us *lives* with a Janara."

Primo's eyes go round. "Are you *serious*? That's fan-*tas*-tic! Does he have any idea who it could—"

"*Sergio!* Where have you been!" his mom yells from outside the back door.

"Right here, Mom!" Sergio hollers. He raises a finger to his lips and goes "*SHHH!*" to Primo.

Mom enters with her usual scowl. Then she sees Primo.

"Oh, Primo!" she says, her whole face changing as she goes to hug him. "My dear, sweet boy, it's so *good* to see you!"

Her gushing mortifies Sergio. Primo is *his* best friend, not hers! Not that Primo seems to mind.

"If I had a son, I'd want him to be just like *you*, Primo!" she says.

"But Mom, you **DO** have a son," Sergio says. "You have seven sons!"

"It's just an expression."

"No, it's not!" Sergio says.

"Hey, what's that smell?" Primo says.

It's coming from Settimo. Or rather, the little yellow puddle Settimo just left on the dirt floor.

"Look at that!" Sergio's mom says. "Sergio! Where are all those diapers I sent you to wash?"

Uh-oh.

Sergio forgot all about the diapers!

He and Primo quickly run—***clop clop clop***, the horns, and *spit!*—down to the river and right to the spot where Sergio left the diapers. But they aren't there!

"So who do you think the Janara could be?" Primo says excitedly.

"Forget about the Janara!" Sergio says. "What happened to the diapers?"

They search and search, but can't find so much as a trace of them.

"This is not going to be good," Primo says, leaving Sergio back at his door.

"*So?*" his mother says, tapping her foot as he comes in. "Where are they? Where are all the diapers?!"

"Uh, I think a Janara took them?" Sergio says. "You know how bad the mischiefs have been...."

Unfortunately, this is not a good excuse. Janara don't steal stuff—they just ruin things—and they never do mischiefs in the middle of the day.

"Now what am I supposed to do? Just let the babies go caca all over the floor?" his mom says. "Do you have any *idea* how much that many diapers cost?"

She throws her hands up in the air and shakes them. She only does this when she's *really* mad.

"You can't do a single simple thing I ask of you," she says, "and yet *every* day, you do exactly what that ghost of yours wants!"

"No, I don't!" Sergio says. "I screw up everything he wants, too! Go ask him—he's always mad at me for getting his orders wrong."

Just when it looks like her eyes are about to pop out of her head, his mom suddenly calms down. Then her face turns sweet.

That is a bad sign.

"You know, dear," she says. "It has become *awfully* crowded in this apartment. I mean, doesn't it just break your heart that your little brothers have to sleep in crates and baskets? And isn't it awful for you to sleep on that table?"

Sergio thinks about getting stabbed in the ribs by the knife this morning, but he doesn't like the way this conversation is going so he just says, "Well, it's not so bad actual—"

"And really, there is so *much* room upstairs. It's just that ghost, after all, and he doesn't even have a body! I really think it would be better for you to move in with him," she says. "Upstairs."

"But, Mom—"

"And then you'll be able to take care of *his* needs more easily, and you will have more time during the day to come down and help *me*."

"But, *Mom*—"

"No buts!" she says, all smiles. "Why, I can't believe I never thought of this before!"

She pushes him out the door and slams it shut with Sergio still *But-Mom*-ing her.

Sergio stands there, unable to believe it. He's nine years old and he just got kicked out of the house. By his own mother!

But that's not the worst part of it. The *worst* part is that now he has to go tell Bis-Bis he's coming to live with him.

BUT, MOM-

"**WHAT?** Your mother told you to **WHAT?**"

Bis-Bis's reaction is even worse than Sergio feared.

"Why, why, why, that's impossible. **Impossible!**" Bis-Bis sputters. "It's that mother of yours—she's **infuriating**! I **TOLD** your father he shouldn't marry her!"

"But if my parents never got married," Sergio says, "then I wouldn't exist."

"Exactly!"

No matter how much he gets insulted, Sergio has to take it. As for why, look no farther than the house next door, which has been abandoned for a hundred years—and all because the family made their ghost mad and she chased them out.

If Sergio doesn't want to wind up sleeping with the rabbits in the garden shed, he has to figure out some way that Bis-Bis will allow him to move in.

He starts by begging.

"Please, *please*, Bis-Bis," he says. "I *promise* I won't be any trouble!"

"**Impossible**, I said!" the ghost says. "I can't have some **child** running around my house all day long."

"I'd mostly just be sleeping here," Sergio says.

"Well, I'm a **night** person," Bis-Bis says, crossing his arms. He farts loudly.

Then Sergio remembers the bag he's carrying.

"I've got your candles," Sergio says. He holds them up and smiles. "The yellow ones, just like you like."

Bis-Bis looks at them, simmering.

"Oh, all right, **FINE!**" Bis-Bis says, throwing up his arms so violently they pop off. "I can't say no to that **stupid** smile. All those **teeth**!" He sits down in his chair and motions toward the corner. "I suppose you can sleep on the floor over there."

"Thank you thank you thank you!" Sergio says. "It's only temporary, I promise! My mom probably wasn't even serious. I mean, *who* would send their nine-year-old boy to go live with a—" Sergio doesn't finish the sentence.

5

CATCH A JANARA
BY THE HAIR

SERGIO thought the table was uncomfortable, but sleeping on the floor is worse. Not that he even slept, not with Bis-Bis knocking and banging around. What does he *do* all night?

Opening the door outside, Sergio allows himself to hope. Maybe his mom really *isn't* serious about making him stay with Bis-Bis. Maybe it's just for one night. To prove a point!

At the bottom of the steps, however, a basket is filled with all of Sergio's clothes. Emilio is standing there looking at it.

"Hey, why is all your stuff out here?" Emilo says, pointing.

Sergio tells him the whole story.

Emilio says he's sorry. "But here." He hands Sergio twenty-three quattrini. "Your half of the mushroom take."

Wow! Sergio thinks, looking at the coins in his hand. He's never had this much money of his *own* before.

"One other thing," Emilio says, lowering his voice. "I should have never told you about . . . y'know. The *secret*. There could be real trouble if anyone finds out."

He looks at Sergio crossways. "You haven't told anybody *else* about it, have you?"

"No," Sergio says, fighting the urge to scratch the back of his neck. "No way."

"Are you *sure*?" Emilio says. "Not even Primo?"

"Definitely not Primo!" Sergio says.

"Thank Plutone," Emilio says. "I just started to get worried. Because what if you did tell Primo? Then *everyone* would know!"

"I told Maria Beppina," Primo says.

"You *what*?!" Sergio says.

Standing next to Primo is Maria Beppina, turning red.

Sergio ran into the two of them at the fountain by the arch, filling up water pails. Before Primo even said anything, Sergio had a sinking feeling.

"I had to tell *somebody* that one of us lives with a Janara," Primo says. "And Maria Beppina is the only person I could trust not to tell anyone *else*. Isn't that right, Maria?"

"Yes," she says, placing a hand on her chest. "I swear!"

Sergio sighs as he fills up his water buckets. "Just make sure Emilio doesn't find out that you know. He'll kill me!"

"Emilio told *me* something," Primo says, his mouth hooking into a smirk. "He said your mom kicked you out of the house and you have to live upstairs with your ghost now."

"Is it true?" Maria Beppina says, genuinely concerned.

Now Sergio tells *them* the whole story.

"But who would steal all those diapers?"

"I have no idea!" Sergio says. "Manalonga?"

"Do Manalonga have babies?" Maria Beppina scrunches her face up, trying to imagine a Manalonga in diapers. "Do they even have bodies?"

"I don't care," Sergio says. He picks up a full bucket in each hand and starts heading home. "All I want is to move back downstairs."

"What are you complaining about?" Primo says. "I'd *love* for my momma to kick me out! No one to tell you when to go to sleep, no one to tell you where to go or what to do at night!"

"But I don't want to *go* anywhere or *do* anything!" Sergio says. "Not at night, anyway."

In front of the bakery, they stop and put down their buckets to give their aching arms a break.

"So I was thinking," Primo says, leaning in and whispering. "If we can figure out *who* the Janara is, we can trap him!"

"Or her," Maria Beppina says.

"Why would we want to do *that*?" Sergio says.

"Because Nonna Jovanna says if you catch a Janara by the hair, they have to grant you seven generations of good luck."

"How can you grab a Janara's hair if they're made of wind?" Maria Beppina says. "Maybe we need a sack to trap them. If only Rosa knew the secret, she could definitely catch one."

"**I** can catch one faster!" Primo says. "Let's go tell her and I'll prove it!"

"No! If we tell Rosa the secret, Emilio will kill me twice!" Sergio says. "Listen, forget about Janara and help me figure out how to get my mom to let me back into the house!"

"I wonder if *she's* the Janara and that's why

she sent you upstairs," Maria Beppina says. "So you won't find out!"

"Or maybe it's your *stepdad* and that's why he never talks!" Primo says.

It makes Sergio's head hurt to think that on top of his living with a ghost, there might be a Janara in his house, too.

"What about *your* family?" Sergio says to Primo. "Nonna Jovanna knows so much about witches, maybe *she's* the Janara."

"Too obvious. Janara have to hide who they are," Primo says. "But maybe it's my *momma*. Or Poppa! That'd be cool."

"How about your sister?" Maria Beppina says.

"Nah," Primo says. "Isidora is too boring to be a witch."

Shaking his head, Sergio picks up his buckets and starts walking again.

"It probably isn't anyone in the Twins' family, otherwise they wouldn't have gotten the mischiefs so bad," Maria Beppina says, following.

"We just need to think of the *most* unlikely person, and *that's* who the Janara has to be," Primo says. "Wait, I got it!" He stops short and spills water everywhere. "It's Maria Beppina's dad!"

"*My* dad?" Maria Beppina says. "But he doesn't even believe witches exist!"

"Exactly! It's the perfect thing to say if you want no one to suspect you!"

"Look, I don't care *who* it is," Sergio says as they arrive in the alley between their homes. "Janara have never given me any trouble. It's mothers and ghosts I need to worry about."

On cue, a shutter from above bangs open. "**Boy!**" Bis-Bis calls, roaring. "Where's that **water**, boy?"

"I'm coming, I'm coming. Hold on!" Sergio says, looking up at Bis-Bis. "You don't have to shout!"

"Is your ghost *really* shouting?" Maria Beppina says.

Other kids can't see or hear Bis-Bis, a fact Sergio always forgets. He only *wishes* he couldn't.

"You left crumbs **everywhere**!" the ghost says. "One night with you and my house is a **pig**sty! Come **clean** this mess up!"

Sergio sighs.

"What does your ghost want?" Maria Beppina says to Sergio as he leaves.

"To make my life miserable," Sergio says.

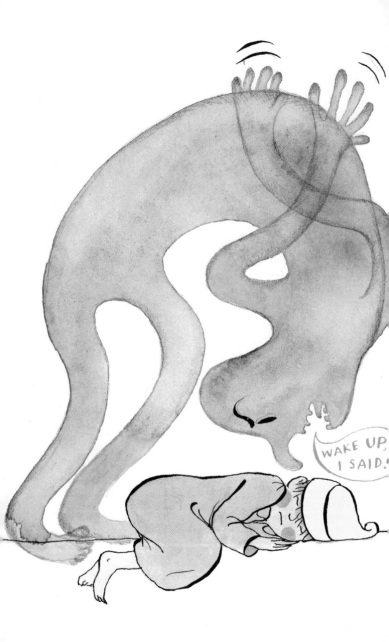

6
VENDETTA

"WILL you wake **up**, boy? **Wake up**, I said!"

It is Bis-Bis, yelling right into Sergio's ear.

"All right, all right, I heard you the first time!" Sergio says, rolling over on the floor. "You sure are *loud* for someone who's dead!"

"And you sure do **sleep** a lot for someone who's alive!"

Sergio sits up and rubs his eyes. It was another night he could barely sleep.

"You told me this was **temporary**!" Bis-Bis says, crossing his arms. "Well, it's been four days, and you're **still** here."

"What can I do?" Sergio says. "Every time I ask my mother if I can move back she pretends like she doesn't hear and gives me something horrible to do. Yesterday, she sent me to the Three Crones!"

Everyone in Benevento is afraid of the Three Crones. Once they gave the evil eye to Gasparro the butcher and all of his hair fell out. Sergio was glad to get the herbs his mom

wanted and get out of there without looking any of the Crones in the eye—and with all his hair on his head—but he's terrified of what his mom will make him do *next*.

"Well, we've got to figure out **something**!" Bis-Bis says.

"Hmm," Sergio says, trying to think.

"Hmm," Bis-Bis says, also trying to think.

The two of them sit there a long time, both trying to think really hard, with nothing happening.

Then Sergio has an idea. "Emilio got the Janara to stop bothering them by doing something nice. Maybe that works with parents, too."

"But you do things for your mother all **day**!" Bis-Bis says.

"Yeah, but something *nice*," Sergio says. "Something she doesn't expect."

"Well, what does she **really** want?"

"Hmm," Sergio says, trying to think.

"Hmm," Bis-Bis says, also trying to think.

Again, this takes a long time.

"I've got it!" Sergio blurts out. "She wants to go to the Carrozzos'. To see her cousin!"

"**No!**" Bis-Bis says. "Absolutely **not**! *Anything* but that!"

Remember that *another* other story? Well, here it is.

The reason Sergio's mom doesn't hate the Carrozzos is that her cousin—and best friend—**is** a Carrozzo. The problem is that the two of them aren't allowed to visit each other, because of the family ghosts.

Once Sergio's mom married into his dad's family and her cousin married into Mozzo's, they had to respect their ghosts, who won't let each other's relatives into their homes.

Bis-Bis and the ghost of the Carrozzos hate each other. Once upon a time *they* were best friends and cousins, but at some point they got into an argument that turned into a vendetta. This vendetta lasted even after the earthquake that killed them both, a hundred and whatever many years ago.

"The Carrozzos' big First of May party is coming up. My mom always talks about how she wishes she could go to it. I bet if she did, she'd be so happy she'd let me come home!" Sergio says. "All it takes is for you and the Carrozzo ghost to make up with each other."

"No! Never!" Bis-Bis shouts. "It will be another hundred and thirty-seven years before I give that Carrozzo what he wants!"

"But *what* does he want?" Sergio says. "What is the vendetta even about?"

No matter how many times Sergio has asked, Bis-Bis has never told him why the feud started.

"And I won't tell you **this** time, either!"

The ghost recrosses his arms and turns his head the other way.

"Was it over a girl?" Sergio says. "Money?"

WAS IT OVER A GIRL?

"No, nothing **silly** like that," Bis-Bis says.

"Then *what*?"

"A **boat**!" Bis-Bis says.

"A boat?" Sergio says. "What kind of boat? A river boat?"

"**No!**" Bis-Bis growls. "A small boat. Made of wood." The ghost puts his hands up a foot apart.

"You mean a *toy* boat?" Sergio says. "You've had a vendetta for one and a half centuries over a *toy*?"

"It is not **just** a toy!" Bis-Bis says. "It's the **principle.** When we were eight, our grandfather gave **each** of us a boat. I took care of mine, which that rotten Carrozzo **stole** after *his* sunk."

"So what does he want?"

"After he stole **my** boat, I went and fished his broken one out of the river. I fixed it up better than **either** of the boats had been in the first place. I put on fresh paint and sewed new sails for it **myself**. You should have **seen** the look on his face when he saw it!" Bis-Bis says triumphantly.

"He **demanded** we trade back. I refused and shut the boat away somewhere no one could ever get at, and he's **hated** me ever since!"

"So you couldn't play with the boat *either*?"

"It was worth it just so he couldn't have the **pleasure**!"

Another thing about vendettas: they are almost *always* stupid.

"So if you give the boat back, will the vendetta be over?" Sergio asks.

The ghost harrumphs.

"Is it still hidden somewhere?"

"**Yes**," Bis-Bis says. "But I'll **never** tell! I've kept that secret for seven generations and I'm **not** giving it up now!"

Bis-Bis is definitely a better secret-keeper than he is, but Sergio *needs* to get that toy boat! He tries asking the ghost where he hid it every way he can think of, without any luck.

"Would you rather keep your vendetta," Sergio finally says, "or be stuck having me live with you for the next ten years?" He smiles.

> FINE! I'LL BE THE BIGGER MAN.

Bis-Bis thinks. His face starts to crack and his eyes move around in their sockets. Finally, he throws up his hands.

"**Fine!**" Bis-Bis shouts. "**I'll** be the bigger man. It's just a stupid **toy**, anyway! Hopefully it's half-**rotten** by now!"

Sergio thanks the ghost as hard as he can.

"But if this doesn't work," Bis-Bis says, wagging a finger at Sergio, "you'll be sleeping with the **rabbits**!"

7
THE BOAT

BEHIND Zia Pia's, rising up from the wide open space where the Clopper runs, stands a small city of workshops. There's the blacksmith's with the black rooster; Zi Totò the tanner's; and down at the bottom, the foul-mouthed brickmaker's. The shops seem to be built on top of each other, but what they are really built on top of are the ancient seats of the Theater.

"We're never gonna find that dumb boat!" Rosa says.

"But Bis-Bis told me **exactly** what to look for," Sergio says.

The ghost put the boat in a hole in one of the brick benches and sealed it up with a slab of marble that had graffiti on it. *It's the picture of a flying donkey with* **wings**, Bis-Bis said.

"Someone probably stole that marble a hundred years ago!" Rosa says. "Or built their workshop on top of it."

"Or maybe it's in the part of the Theater that collapsed," Emilio says, pointing. He heads down to inspect the rubble and tall grass.

"I bet it's up behind the blacksmith's," Primo says, starting to climb. "I'm going to check!"

"Well, I'm not going anywhere!" Rosa says, and plops herself down on an old seat. "If I wanted to work this hard I'd have stayed home!"

The work is in clearing the old benches, overgrown as they are with weeds and brush, to look for the picture of the flying donkey.

"Hey, I found it!" Primo shouts. "The drawing!

Sergio comes up to look, but even with his eyes he can see that the scratches Primo is pointing at are not what they're looking for. "That's not a donkey. That's not even a drawing!"

"I know," Primo says, whispering. "I just wanted to ask if Emilio gave you any other hints about who the Janara is."

"Shh!" Sergio shushes Primo. "Do you want him to hear!?"

"I tried to trick my momma into admitting she was a Janara and she got all angry."

"Seriously, stop! Emilio is right over—"

"Hey, what're you guys whispering about?" Rosa says, coming up behind them. "What's the big secret?"

Emilio stops digging to look up at them.

"No secret!" Sergio says, loud enough so Emilio can hear. "We weren't even whispering!"

"Yeah, you're hearing things," Primo says to Rosa. "It must be all that gross wax in your ears."

"Shut your mouth, donkey-brains!"

"Why don't you *make* me!"

"Guys, please!" Maria Beppina says as Primo and Rosa start to wrestle.

Rosa slips on a rock and falls on her butt to the rubble, causing a small landslide. A chunk of white stone goes tumbling and falls at Emilio's feet.

"Hey, guys!" Emilio says. "I think Rosa's butt just found what we're looking for."

The kids stand over the marble, looking at the picture of a winged donkey.

"I guess the boat *was* in the part of the Theater that fell down," Primo says.

Sergio is devastated.

"*Now* what am I going to do?"

"Do about what, boy?"

DO ABOUT WHAT, BOY?

Startled, the kids jump and turn to see . . .

Amerigo Pegleg!

Where did he *come* from? It was like he appeared out of thin air.

"What are you kiddies poking around for?"

"We're looking for a boat," Primo says.

"Shouldn't you be a-looking in the river, then?" Amerigo says.

"It's not that kind of boat," Sergio says, and explains the whole story. Well, most of it.

"A *toy* boat, eh?" Amerigo says, a smile coming to his face. He rubs his stubbly chin. "I think I might just be able to help you kiddies. But first I have to ask: Can you keep a secret?"

Amerigo puts his arm on Emilio's shoulder. Emilio almost looks scared.

"Sure, we can keep a secret!" Primo says. "We're fan-*tas*-tic secret-keepers!"

CAN YOU KEEP A SECRET?

Amerigo takes the kids inside his one-room hovel beneath Zia Pia's.

"I grew up in this Theater!" Amerigo says, dipping a torch in black pitch. "When I was no older than you all, I discovered the ancient passageways and chambers within. It's a secret world that only *I* know!" He sets the torch on fire with a hiss. "And we enter it through *here*!"

"Here" is an oversized mousehole in the back wall. Amerigo crawls through it—he's surprisingly spry—and leads the kids into a maze of tunnels.

Can the boat *really* be somewhere in this spooky underworld? All Sergio wants is to get OUT of here!

Finally, they come to the end of the labyrinth. Out the other side, they enter into a place that none of the kids can believe.

"It's like a palace!" Maria Beppina says.

Lighting a series of torches, Amerigo reveals a great underground hall. All around are bits of statues and columns, decorated with the feathers, glass beads, and other trinkets Amerigo sells.

IT'S LIKE A PALACE!

"I call it my Museum of Extra-Ordinary Artifacts," Amerigo says. "And here is one of my most *extra*-extra-ordinary pieces." He bows and sweeps his arms like a puppeteer presenting his show.

It is the boat.

It is beautiful.

Its keel is painted yellow and the sails are white. Some of the paint is chipping, and the fabric is frayed in places, but it's amazing how good it looks after all this time.

"When the north side of the Theater collapsed, I found her sitting at the bottom of a cascade of rubble, like she had come a-sailing down it. I always wondered where she came from." Amerigo says, lifting the boat from its place. "A vendetta! I should've known . . ."

Mozzo is suspicious from the moment the five of them set foot in the stable. "What do you losers want?"

"It's not what *we* want," Primo says, "it's what your *ghost* wants."

"What's this moron talking about, moron?" Mozzo says, turning to Emilio, who in turn turns to Sergio.

"My ghost wants to end the family vendetta," Sergio says.

"Oh, *yeah*?" says Catina, who is one of Mozzo's sisters. She is—if possible—even more of a jerk than Mozzo. "And what's he gonna do about it?"

"Give your ghost what he wants, just like Primo said," Sergio says. "The boat."

Both Carrozzos screw their faces up into the same snarling, confused expression.

"What boat?" Mozzo says. "What does our ancestor want with a boat?"

"Just tell your ghost about the boat," Rosa says, thumping a finger in Mozzo's chest.

"It's a lovely boat," Maria Beppina says.

Mozzo and his sister whisper in each other's ears. "We have to go talk to our ancestor," Catina says, and they disappear out the back for what seems like forever.

When they finally get back, Catina says, "And what does your ghost want in return?"

"To let my mom come to your First of May feast," Sergio says.

More confused expressions, whispering, and another long trip out the back later, Catina says, "If you do return *his* boat, our generous ancestor will allow your mother to come to the First of May feast."

"But if this is some kind of trick, then **BAM**!" Mozzo says, punching his own palm. "You losers are dead."

Stepping over to him, Rosa looks down threateningly. "The same goes for you," she says. "There'll be *two* Carrozzo ghosts if you don't hold up your end of the deal."

Mozzo keeps smiling, but it's a phony, scared kind of smile. Sergio is sure glad Rosa is on *his* side!

8

THE HOUSE OF CARROZZO

SHOES! How can people *wear* these things?

Of course, having a pair that fit might help. The ones Sergio is wearing—the first shoes he's *ever* worn—were borrowed by his mother from someone two years younger than him and a foot shorter.

She thinks the shoes will help Sergio make a good impression at the feast. But how can Sergio make a good impression if he can't even walk?

"Har-hu-har-har-HAR!" Bis-Bis roars as he watches Sergio hobble around in pain. "I haven't laughed this *hu-har-har-HARD* in a hundred years!"

Sergio has never heard his ghost laugh before. Now he wishes he never had.

"Oh, I don't even **care** about that boat anymore!" Bis-Bis says, wiping a tear from his cheek. "This makes it **completely** worth it!"

Down the steps, it's all Sergio can do not to fall and crack the boat (not to mention his skull). Inside with his mom and stepfather are Emilio and Maria Beppina, who are going to babysit his brothers, and Rosa and Primo, who are coming with Sergio to face the Carrozzos.

Walking in, Sergio stumbles.

"Hey, watch it!" Primo says, grabbing the boat out of his hands. "We still have to give this thing to Mozzo!"

"Oh, how sweet of you to be bringing him a present!" Sergio's mom says, patting Primo's arm. "Mozzo's a very *nice* boy, really."

The kids all trade looks.

Sergio hasn't told his mom that the boat is the reason she got invited to the Carrozzos'. He doesn't want her blaming *him* for not being able to see her cousin if something goes wrong.

"Thank goodness those ghosts have finally gotten over what*ever* their silly vendetta was!" his mom says, primping in a mirror.

"That's a nice fancy dress, Zia!" Primo says.

"You are too kind! Too kind!" She half twirls on her toes and pretends to blush.

Primo and Rosa each take Sergio's mom by an arm and start out the door, with Sergio and his stepfather trailing up the rear.

The walk up the hill suddenly seems *so* long. With every step—*ouch, ouch, ouch*—Sergio gets farther behind.

"Hurry up!" his mom yells from ahead. "I don't want to be late!

The Carrozzo house stands at the top of the Triggio just below the arch, right where the paving stones—and the rich part of town—begin. The Carrozzo house itself

is the fanciest one in the
Triggio. So fancy, in fact, that
it has stairs on the *inside* of the house.

Sergio's mom takes a deep breath as she
comes to the door. She nods, walks in, and
then freezes as she and her cousin lock eyes
from across the room. They've passed each
other on the street a million times, but they've
avoided looking at each other since their
trouble began.

Remembering herself, Sergio's mom grabs
her dress and does a grand bowing curtsy. At

that moment, Zia Carrozzo leaps up and hugs her. The two of them start to cry.

Sergio feels good for his mom, and so do Primo and Rosa. The good feelings vanish, however, when Mozzo and his sister come walking over.

"*This* is the boat?" Mozzo says with a sour look as he takes it out of Primo's hands.

"I don't know if our ancestor's going to like this..." Catina says, and turns to leave.

"Wait here, losers," Mozzo says, following her.

"No problem," Primo says. His sniffing nose turns toward the boar being roasted on the other side of the room.

"You think we're gonna get some of that food?" Rosa says to Sergio, licking her lips.

"I have no idea," Sergio says. The way his stomach feels, the last thing he wants to do is eat.

This time, Mozzo and Catina come back quickly. They don't have the boat.

"Our ancestor wants to see you," Catina says.

"Uh, okay," Sergio says. "But how can we see *him*?"

Don't they know you can only see your *own* house spirit?

"Just come on, moron," Mozzo says.

They walk through the back of the house into a courtyard, on the other side of which sits a rear house set into a hidden garden.

"In here," Mozzo says, walking to the back building.

Sergio follows Mozzo, but his sister puts up an arm to block Primo and Rosa.

"Just him," Catina says.

"Wait, why can't they come?" Sergio asks.

"Because our ancestor said so," she says.

"You aren't *scared*, are you?" Mozzo says.

"No way he's scared!" Rosa says. "He *lives* with a ghost."

"Don't worry," Primo says, waving Sergio on. "We'll be right here waiting if these Carrozzos try anything!"

The thing is, Sergio *is* scared. In fact, he's terrified. Yes, he lives with a ghost, but what's that got to do with meeting a *different* ghost? On the other hand, he won't be able to see the ghost—or even hear him—so maybe it won't be so scary after all.

But just the darkness is scary! Because it is really, *really* dark inside the little back house. Only the tiniest bit of light comes creeping through the edges of the old, crooked shutters.

His eyes start to adjust, however, and that's when Sergio *does* see the ghost, seated in the middle of the room like a king on a throne.

But how can that be? It breaks every rule of ancestor spirits!

The freaky thing— the thing that makes the hair on the back of Sergio's neck stand up—is that under the hat there is no face.

9

BELOVED ANCESTORS

SERGIO could run. In fact, every bone in his body is telling him to do just that. But then Sergio realizes that he *doesn't* see the Carrozzo ghost. What he's looking at is an empty suit of clothes.

The hat turns to Mozzo's sister, who is nodding along as if being spoken to. Catina *is* being spoken to, Sergio realizes—he just can't hear what the ghost is saying. Now he knows what other kids feel like.

"Our beloved ancestor says to tell you that he wanted to see you, and he dressed like this so you could see *him*," Catina says.

"Uh, thank you?" Sergio says, looking into

where he imagines the spirit's eyes are.

The well-dressed ghost lifts a glove, beckoning Sergio to come closer.

"Go on, dummy," Mozzo says, pushing Sergio.

"He wants you to shake his hand," Catina says. "To seal the end of the vendetta."

The white glove of the Carrozzo ghost feels soft at first. Then the ghost grips Sergio's hand so hard it hurts, making the handshake creepy *and* painful.

The hat of the ghost again turns toward Catina. As she nods along silently, Sergio notices the boat, laid out on a table beside the ghost.

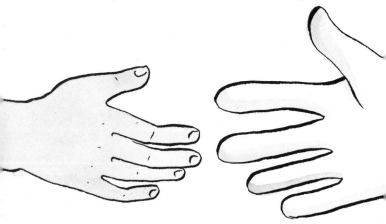

"Our beloved ancestor says that he wants you to know the *true* story of the boat," she says, "as he is sure your ancestor must have lied to you."

The ghost draws his gloved fingers together in the gesture meaning *Do you understand?*

Sergio nods.

"Our beloved ancestor says that both of the boats belonged to him, and that he only allowed your ancestor to *borrow* one. Naturally, when this one sank, he wanted the other one back."

The ghost points at Catina for emphasis.

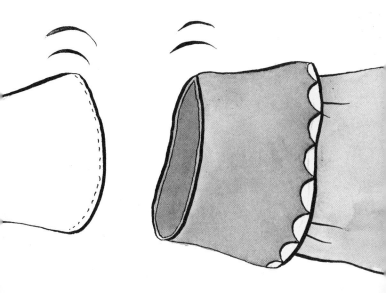

"Before he could fix the broken boat, your ancestor took it upon himself to try. It was infuriating! Just look at what a bad job he did!"

"It looks pretty good to me," Sergio says. "Especially after a hundred and forty years."

The ghost grabs the brim of his hat and looks to the ceiling, then turns to Catina.

"Good? Why look at this color! Yellow? Who paints their boat yellow? And these burlap sails—they look ridiculous! It was just like him to do a sloppy, terrible job on *everything*. Even his own mother was always complaining about how lazy and stupid he was!"

"Well, mothers can be wrong about stuff like that," Sergio mutters.

"No! He was a little fool is what he was!" The gestures of the ghost fly

more furiously as he leans forward menacingly toward Sergio. Mozzo, standing off to the side, smiles his widest smile.

"And another thing," Catina goes on as the ghost wags a white-gloved finger. "Tell that ancestor of yours that it's a sign of how **forgiving** our beloved ancestor is that he is even willing to let that low-born, ill-mannered woman into our house."

That's it! Insulting his ghost is one thing. But insulting his mother!

AND ANOTHER THING...

"If I may talk now," Sergio says. "I have a message from *my* beloved ancestor to *you*."

"Oh yes?" The Carrozzo ghost settles back into his chair. "What is it?"

"**This!**" Sergio says, and gives him the hardest flick of a two-handed mundza he can muster.

Mozzo and Catina look stunned. The ghost is motionless. Then his gloves grasp at the air like he's strangling someone.

"You can't do that to our beloved ancestor!" Catina says.

"Yeah! And in his own house!" Mozzo says. "Who do you think you are!"

"Alive or dead, you Carrozzos are all the same!" Sergio says. **"Jerks!"**

Then he turns and races away, pushing

through the door right past Rosa and Primo.

"What's going on?" Primo yells after him.

Rosa doesn't wait for an answer. She sticks out a leg to trip Mozzo as he comes tearing out of the back house. His older sister, right on his heels, goes tumbling over him.

In the middle of the courtyard, Sergio looks back to see what's happening, and *he* trips—over these stupid shoes!

Rosa and Primo each pull him up by an arm and the three of them hurry into the front house just a step ahead of the Carrozzos.

Inside, Mozzo's father is making a toast.

". . . and as we welcome the rebirth of Nature on this happy First of May, let us also welcome the rebirth of friendships." He raises his glass toward Sergio's mother. *"Salut!"*

"Salut!" the adults all say, raising their own glasses.

Primo turns to Mozzo and Catina and gives them the chicken peck—*Suckers!*

Mozzo answers with a hand chop to his head— *I'm going to GET you!*

"Sergio, my dear boy!" his mother calls to him. She's holding out her hands for a hug.

His feet more in pain than ever, Sergio hobbles over to where she is sitting and smiling with her cousin and two other ladies. They all laugh.

"Take those shoes off, dear!" his mom says. "We *must* buy you a new pair!"

"Okay," Sergio says, and kicks them off.

"I *miss* you, dear!" his mom says. "Why haven't you been sleeping at home?"

"Uh, because you told me to go sleep up with the ghost," Sergio says.

"Oh, that's just an expression! I wasn't *serious!*" his mom says, and she and the other ladies laugh again. "Come back downstairs, you silly boy!"

His mom gives Sergio a big kiss and goes back to her friends. Sergio heads over to look for Primo and Rosa and finds them at the buffet table. His stepfather is there, too, and all three of them are stuffing chunks of roast boar into their mouths, shirts, and pockets.

"Come on!" Sergio whispers to Rosa and Primo. "Let's sneak out of here before anything *else* can go wrong."

Outside, they start walking down the hill, stepping off the cold, hard paving stones onto the warm soft dirt of the Triggio street.

It feels so good.

10
HOME SWEET HOME

"ARE you **serious**? Are you **sure**?" Bis-Bis says. "Your mother is really letting you move back downstairs?"

"Yes!" Sergio says. "The plan worked *perfectly*!"

Except for Mozzo and his sister and ghost now wanting to kill him, that is. But Sergio isn't going to mention that part.

"What **joy**, my boy!" Bis-Bis says, throwing his arms around Sergio.

Sergio finishes packing all of his clothes into a box. "Well, I'll see you in the morning for your offering!" he says.

"Oh, don't **worry** about the offering!" Bis-Bis says. "Why don't you take tomorrow off?"

"Okay," Sergio says, hardly able to believe it. Bis-Bis has *never* given him a day off.

Sergio is half out the door when Bis-Bis stops him.

"One other thing," the ghost says. "That old so-and-so . . ." Bis-Bis pauses, a hint of worry on his face. "Did he say anything about me?"

"Uh . . ." Sergio thinks for a moment. "He said you were very forgiving." Sergio scratches the back of his neck. "And raised a glass to a re-birth of friendship."

"**Hah!** He did, **did** he?" Bis-Bis claps and rubs his hands. As Sergio leaves, the ghost happily calls after him, "Why don't you take the whole **week** off?"

Carrying his basket of clothes back downstairs, Sergio can't believe it. Everything works out. For once!

The next morning, Sergio feels as free as a bird. He runs across the street to Primo's and finds Emilio there. He asks Sergio if he wants to go hunting with them.

"Sure!" Sergio says. "Without offerings to make, I can do whatever I want!"

"Don't you still have to check with your mom first?" Emilio says.

"Oh, dang!" Sergio says. "Right."

Back home, Sergio notices that all of his brothers have runny noses and are sneezing. Settimo looks especially bad. He doesn't even have his toes in his mouth.

"There you are!" Sergio's mother says happily. "How *nice* it is to have you home, son!"

She comes and gives him a kiss, then puts on her fanciest head scarf.

"Why are you so dressed up?" Sergio says.

"I'm going to get my hair combed, like a proper lady! Things are different now," she says. "Aren't you happy for me?"

"Sure," Sergio says. "I guess."

"I will be gone most of the day, so you have to mind your brothers."

"Oh," Sergio says. "I was kind of hoping I could go hunting."

"The new diapers are in the chest," his mother says, as if Sergio had said nothing at all. "And the little ones still need their breakfast. And make sure that every half hour you suck the snot out of the baby's nose."

Sergio laughs.

"Why are you laughing?"

"Because you're kidding about sucking out the snot, right?" Sergio says. "*Right?*"

"He's too little to blow his own nose. You don't want him to suffocate, do you?" his mother says, pausing at the door. "I did it for you when *you* were a baby."

And she leaves.

Sergio is terrified to be alone with Settimo. Yellow-green gook is smeared from the baby's nose across his cheeks, and with every breath out, a snot bubble forms from his left nostril.

"Primo!" Sergio yells across the street. "Primo! You have to get over here RIGHT NOW!"

"What's going on?" Primo says when he gets there. "We were just about to leave without you."

"You can't leave me here!" Sergio says, and explains the situation.

"*Skeevo!*" Primo says. "That can't *really* be true. What baby ever suffocated on its own snot?"

It does seem like Settimo is having trouble breathing, though. The snot bubble is getting smaller and smaller.

"Hey!" Emilio calls from outside. "Are you two coming or what?"

"You've gotta help us!" Sergio yells. "We've got a crisis here."

After hearing the situation, Emilio says, "The Janara stuck a straw up Rosa's nose to suck all the food out of her stomach. Maybe the same thing works with snot."

"Geez," Primo says. "If only we knew who the Janara was, we could ask them to do it *for* us!"

Uh-oh.

Emilio becomes so mad it looks like his cap is going to pop off.

"How could you *tell* him?" he says to Sergio. "You **promised**!"

"Hey, don't get mad at me!" Sergio says. "Everyone *knows* I can't keep a secret!"

Emilio turns to Primo. "And who did *you* tell?"

"No one!" Primo says. "Only Maria Beppina. I swear!"

At that moment, a horrible cough comes from Settimo.

"You have to do something, Sergio," Primo says.

"I have a straw," Emilio says, reaching into one of his pockets.

"No way!" Sergio says. "Even with a straw, I'll *still* be sucking snot into my mouth!"

"How about we use *this*?" Primo says, grabbing the bellows from above the fireplace.

"But that's for blowing air *on*to a fire," Sergio says. "Not sucking it in."

"You have to suck the air in to start," Primo

says. He demonstrates by placing the nozzle against Sergio's arm and opening the bellows. It pulls his skin inside.

"Ow!" Sergio says.

"It's worth a try," Emilio says.

While Primo holds the bellows and Emilio holds Settimo, Sergio tries guiding the nozzle into the baby's left nostril, but it's no good. His nose is too small.

"I don't know," Primo says. "I think you have to do it. You have to suck the snot out."

"Yeah, you have to." Emilio says. "It's getting worse."

Sergio is saved for a moment, however, as the front door bangs open again.

It's Rosa.

"I can't believe that everyone else knew that one of us is living with a Janara except me!" she says to Emilio. "Your own twin!"

"You *did* tell her!" Emilio says, turning to Primo.

"No, I didn't!" he says.

"Actually, he didn't," Rosa says, and turns to Maria Beppina, walking through the door.

NO, I DIDN'T!

I HAD TO TELL SOMEONE!

Her face turns red. "I had to tell *some*one!" Maria Beppina says.

"So who *is* the Janara, anyway?" Rosa says.

"No one knows! But forget that for now," Primo says. "Sergio's about to suck the snot out of the baby's nose! It's going to be fan-*tas*-tic!"

"*No!*" Maria Beppina says.

"**Skeevo!**" Rosa says.

We wish we could end the story here, and leave Sergio with some shred of dignity intact.

But we can't.

Life goes on, but our book is done!

So it seems that parents need respect every bit as much as ghosts, or they may turn you out of the house as well. I would say that Sergio has learned a valuable lesson, except I am not sure that Sergio learns lessons. Too bad.

If nothing else, the boy at least has learned some valuable questions. The answer to one—Who helped Emilio?—you may already know, if you have been reading along with us.

You may even know that some of the things Sergio does not question—such as the "magic" of Primo's ring, or Maria Beppina having been "caught"—are not quite as they seem.

The other, more explosive riddle—Who is the Janara?—will only be

Revealed with time. If you, however, are a CAREFUL reader, perhaps you can find the answer to this as well.

If you've read the first four books, perhaps it is time that you read them again!

Sigismondo
RAFAELLA
BRUNO

S.   R.   B.

SPEAKING WITH HANDS

FOR thousands of years, the people of southern Italy have used their hands to help them speak. Until very recently this was necessary because languages changed from one town to the next—sometimes from one *neighborhood* to the next. The language of the hands, however, was universal.

1. **The Eye:** This is a warning. *Pay attention!*

2. **The Marameo:** For making fun of somebody. *Na-nuh-na-na-NA-na!*

3a. **The One-Handed Mundza:**
For insulting somebody.
You idiot!

3b. **The Two-Handed Mundza:**
For starting a vendetta with
somebody. *You $*&#!*

4. **The Pazzo:** This is especially
good for little brothers. *You're
driving me crazy!*

5. **The Word of Honor:** For
promises. *I swear!*

6. **The Horns:** Gestures aren't
only for speaking! This sign
wards off trickster sprites, evil
eyes, and most of your everyday
bad magic. *Puh-tooey!*

Life was very different in Benevento in the 1820s.

HERE'S HOW THEY LIVED.

- Could kids read? No way! Not many of them, anyway. Their parents couldn't read either. Reading was considered weird.

- Eyeglasses were rare. Since folks couldn't read anyway, there wasn't much point.

- Shoes were only for fancy people.

- Stairs were on the outside of houses, even if the same family lived on both floors.

- Not only did many people never live anywhere but the home they were born in, many families stayed in the same home for generation upon generation. This was very convenient for ancestor ghosts.

- There was no electricity. For light, you used a candle or an oil lamp.

- Houses didn't have water, either. To get some, you needed to take a bucket to a well or fountain. To wash clothes, you went to the river. Oh, and if you needed to use a toilet, you had to go outside for that, too!

- Going back to Roman times, parents often gave their kids a number for a name. A first-born boy might be called Primo. The fifth, sixth, and seventh born might be Quinto, Sessimo, and Settimo.

- Most people had only two outfits: fancy suits for feasts, and the clothes they wore every other day of the year.

If you want to learn MORE, please visit www.witchesofbenevento.com.

HISTORICAL NOTE

—✦—

THE WITCHES OF BENEVENTO is set in 1820s Benevento.

Benevento was an important crossroads in Roman times and was the capital of the Lombards in Southern Italy during the early Middle Ages.

Even before the Romans conquered it, the town was famous as a center of witches. (Its original name, Maleventum—"bad event"—was switched by the Romans to Beneventum—"good event"—in hope of changing things. It didn't work.) For hundreds of years, Benevento was believed to be the place where all the witches of the world gathered, attending their peculiar festivals at a walnut tree near the Sabato River.

The people of Benevento, however, never believed there was anything wrong with witches, and maybe that's why they had—or thought they had—so many of them.

JOHN BEMELMANS MARCIANO

I grew up on a farm taking care of animals. We had one spectacularly nice chicken, the Missus, who lived in a stall with an ancient horse named Gilligan, and one rooster, Leon, who pecked our heads on our way home from school. Leon, I have no doubt, was a demon. Presently I take care of two cats, one dog, and a daughter.

SOPHIE BLACKALL

I've illustrated many books for children, including the Ivy and Bean series. I drew the pictures in this book using ink made from black olives and goat spit. This year, I received a shiny gold Caldecott Medal for *Finding Winnie*. I grew up in Australia, but now my boyfriend and I live in Brooklyn with a cat who never moves and a bunch of children who come and go like the wind.

Read the other books in the

WITCHES of BENEVENTO
series!

MISCHIEF SEASON:
A Twins Story

Emilio and Rosa are tired of all the nasty tricks the
Janara are playing when they ride at night making
mischiefs. Maybe the fortune-teller Zia Pia
will know how to stop the witches.

THE ALL-POWERFUL RING:
A Primo Story

Primo wants to prove he is the bravest, but will the
ring really protect him from all danger—even from
the Manalonga, who hide in wells and under bridges?

BEWARE THE CLOPPER!
A Maria Beppina Story

Maria Beppina, the timid tagalong cousin, is also the slow-
est runner of the five. She is always afraid that the Clopper, the old witch who chases the children, will catch her.
She's also curious, so one day she decides to stop—just
stop—and see what the Clopper will do.